EVERYONE LOVES THE MOON

ALSO BY JAMES YOUNG

A Million Chameleons
Penelope and the Pirates

Copyright © 1991 by James Young

First North American Edition 1992

First published in Great Britain in 1991 by Collins Children's
Division, a division of HarperCollins Publishers

ISBN 0-316-97130-8

Library of Congress Catalog Card Number 90-27456

Library of Congress Cataloging-in-Publication data
is available.

10 9 8 7 6 5 4 3 2 1

Published simultaneously in Canada
by Little, Brown & Company (Canada) Limited

Printed in the People's Republic of China

EVERYONE LOVES THE MOON

James Young

 Little, Brown and Company
Boston—Toronto—London

The night is dark; the woods are deep.
You think that everyone's asleep.
But there's a cricket, a cow, a cat.
Where's the bear? Was that a bat?
And here's a possum and a raccoon.
Everyone loves the moon.

Mr. Raccoon and Ms. O'Possum
Strolled beneath the cherry blossoms.
Mr. Raccoon knelt and said,
"My dear Ms. O'Possum, let us be wed."
"Oh, I cannot, Mr. Raccoon,
For I only love the moon."

Cows love the moon, no one knows why.
Night after night, they stare at the sky.
Night after night, they look above
And sing their nightly song of love.
"Mooooon, mooooon," cows sweetly croon.
"Everyone loves the moooooooooon."

"Ms. O'Possum, be my bride.
We'll row through life, dear, side by side."
"Why, Mr. Raccoon, I do declare,
I'd let you row me anywhere.
Even around this old lagoon.
But I only love the moon."

A bear tried to catch the moon in his net
But found only fish — shiny and wet.
He reached for the moon with every cast,
Thinking the moon was his at last.
But still she glows like a gold doubloon.
Everyone loves the moon.

Ms. O'Possum and Mr. Raccoon
Floated in a blue balloon.
"Oh, look down there, Ms. O'Possum,
Isn't it lovely? Isn't it awesome?"
"It may be that, dear Mr. Raccoon,
But I only love the moon."

They saw a cat lost in a dream.
She dreamed that the moon
Was a bowl of sweet cream.
And to get every drop,
She used a spoon.
Everyone loves the moon.

All night long the cricket sings
His song of the moon (and other things).
"Oh, the moon comes up, the moon goes down.
The stars keep spinning round and round.
The stars are spinning over the sea,
Over the land and over me.
And all night long I fiddle a tune.
Everyone loves the moon."

While strolling through the woods one night,
Mr. Raccoon saw a wonderful sight.
"My dear Ms. O'Possum, I beg your pardon.
I've never seen such a lovely garden."
"Well, Mr. Raccoon, between us two,
I only plant when the moon is new.
It makes the seeds come up quite soon.
Everyone loves the moon."

In hopes Ms. O'Possum would wear his ring,
Mr. Raccoon began to sing.
"Take your fiddle, raise your bow.
The moon is back; we missed her so.
Strum the guitar, thrum the bass.
The moon is back in her own place.
Bang the banjo, honk the bassoon.
Everyone loves the moon."

"Why, Mr. Raccoon, what a lovely song.
I could listen all night long."
"My dear Ms. O'Possum, you're very kind.
I'll sing it again, if you don't mind.
It's just a simple little tune
Called 'Everyone Loves the Moon.'

"Each night the moon comes over the hill.
She always has; she always will.
We know because we always wait.
Sometimes she's early; sometimes she's late.
But whether late or whether soon,
Everyone loves the moon.

"Ms. O'Possum, do be mine.
Here beneath the bright moonshine."
"You've won my heart at last," she cried.
"Mr. Raccoon, I'll be your bride.
Let us be wed and let it be soon.
Everyone loves the moon."

O'Possum and Raccoon were wed
When the moon was overhead.
Every bird and every beast
Gathered for their wedding feast
On a lovely night in June.
Everyone loves the moon.